IMAGINE THAT

Licensed exclusively to Imagine That Publishing Ltd
Tide Mill Way, Woodbridge, Suffolk, IP12 1AP, UK
www.imaginethat.com
Copyright © 2019 Imagine That Group Ltd
All rights reserved
0 2 4 6 8 9 7 5 3 1
Manufactured in China

Written by Susie Linn
Illustrated by Natalia Moore

ISBN 978-1-78700-899-1

A catalogue record for this book is available from the British Library

'For Sarah, always an angel.' SL

What an Angel!

Written by Susie Linn

Illustrated by Natalia Moore

Mum and Grandma gazed down at the new baby.

'Isn't she sweet?
Isn't she adorable?'
sighed Mum.

'What an angel!' whispered Grandma.

'That's it!' said Mum.
'That's what I'm going to call her ... Angel!'

But Mum and Grandma were in for a surprise.

On the day of the Beautiful Baby Contest, 'sweet', 'adorable' Angel was tired of waiting for her turn.

BLIP ... BLOP ... BLOOP ...
went the lovely, gloopy mud,
as Angel made her first mud pie ever.

'Tee-hee-hee-hee-hee,'
giggled Angel, happily.

At Angel's friend Daisy's fifth birthday party,
all the little girls were busy decorating cupcakes with
sweeties and delicate sugar sprinkles. All except for Angel.

'... Seven, eight, nine ...' counted Angel,
as she built her very own sweet-treat tower,
sandwiching the cupcakes together with lots of squidgy icing.

'Ten!' squealed Angel, as her tower teetered ... tottered ... and fell over!

One Saturday, Grandma took Angel shopping to buy some pretty pink ballet shoes.

But Angel had a different plan.

'Wow!' cried Angel, stomping around the shop in a pair of big, shiny, red boots.

At school, Angel loved science most of all.

While the other children worked quietly,
doing their neat science experiments,
Angel was busy with an experiment of her own.

'Angel ... how about learning to play a musical instrument?' suggested Mum one day. 'Like the recorder, or maybe the flute?' she said, hopefully.

One week later ... KERRRANG! KERCHANG! KERTWANG! went Angel's electric guitar, as she ran her hand over the strings.

Everyone despaired of Angel, but Angel was very happy just being herself.

It was almost the end of term when Angel spotted a poster on the school noticeboard.

The evening of the Fame-factor Talent Contest arrived.
Group after group of children took to the stage.

They played
piano duets ...

acted out scenes from plays ...

sang ...

played the recorder ...

read poems ...

and told jokes.

Then, at long last,
it was Angel's turn.

The lights went down and the curtain went up.

There was a loud KERRRANG! ... and Angel,
in her red boots and denims, with her wild, wild hair,
took to the stage with her electric guitar.

And she was AMAZING!

'Angel! Angel! Angel!'
the audience yelled in excitement.

The guest judge was as impressed as the audience.

'And the first prize goes to ... ANGEL!'

'YES!' cried Angel, jumping up and down.

Being herself was just GREAT!

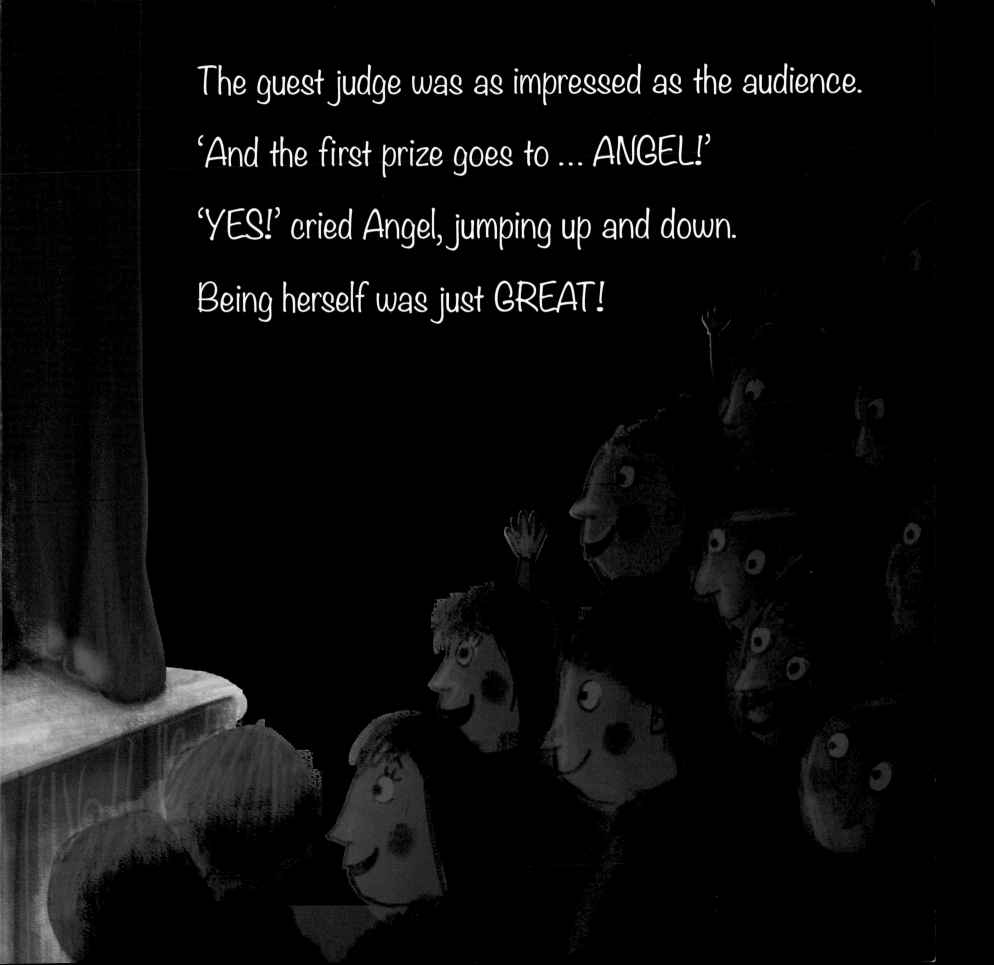

Just the beginning ...